TEEN TITANS GO!™

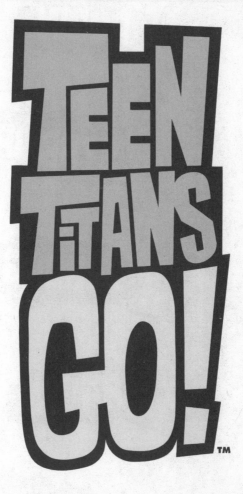

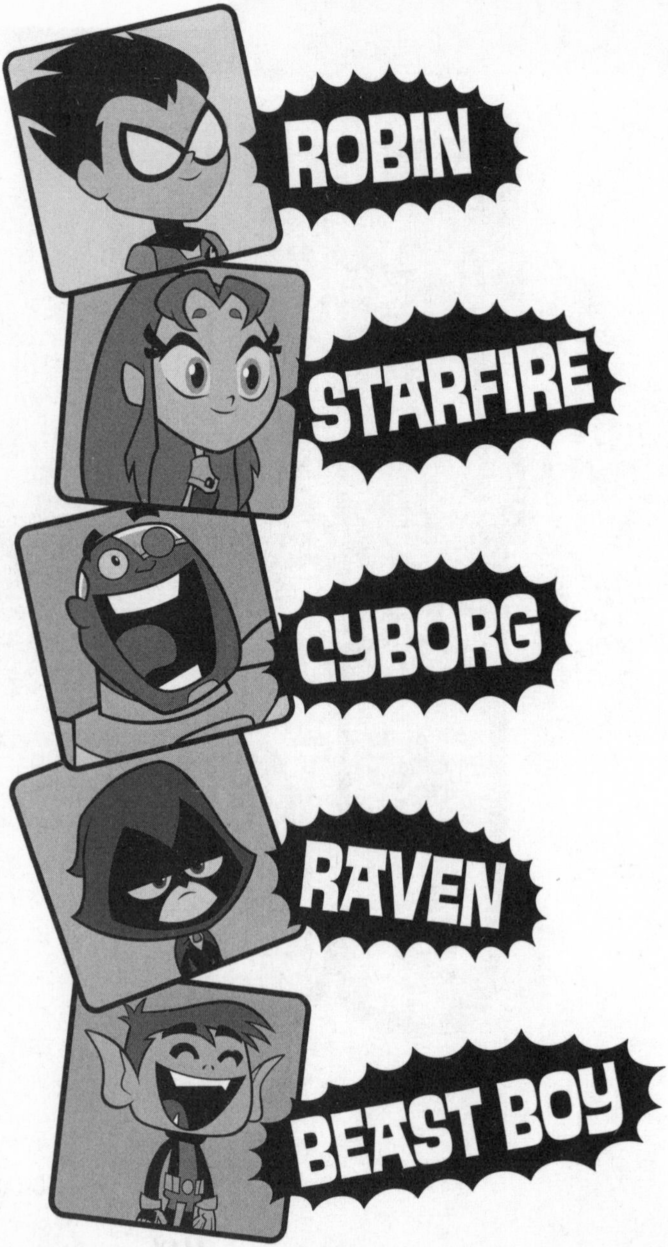
ROBIN
STARFIRE
CYBORG
RAVEN
BEAST BOY

TEEN TITANS GO!™

GAME TIME

Adapted by **Steve Korté**

Based on the episodes

"Video Game References" by

Michael Jelenic & Aaron Horvath

"Riding the Dragon" by **Will Friedle**

"Kicking a Ball and Pretending to Be Hurt"

by **Michael Jelenic & Aaron Horvath**

LITTLE, BROWN AND COMPANY

New York   Boston

Copyright © 2017 DC Comics.
TEEN TITANS GO! and all related characters and elements
© & ™ DC Comics and Warner Bros. Entertainment Inc.
(s17)

Cover design by Ching Chan and Carolyn Bull

Little, Brown and Company
Hachette Book Group
1290 Avenue of the Americas, New York, NY 10104
Visit us at lb-kids.com

First Edition: November 2017

Little, Brown and Company is a division of Hachette Book Group, Inc.
The Little, Brown name and logo are trademarks of Hachette Book Group, Inc.

The publisher is not responsible for websites
(or their content) that are not owned by the publisher.

Library of Congress Control Number 2017944466

ISBNs: 978-0-316-50682-3 (pbk.), 978-0-316-50681-6 (ebook)

PRINTED IN THE UNITED STATES OF AMERICA

LSC-C

10 9 8 7 6 5 4 3 2

CONTENTS

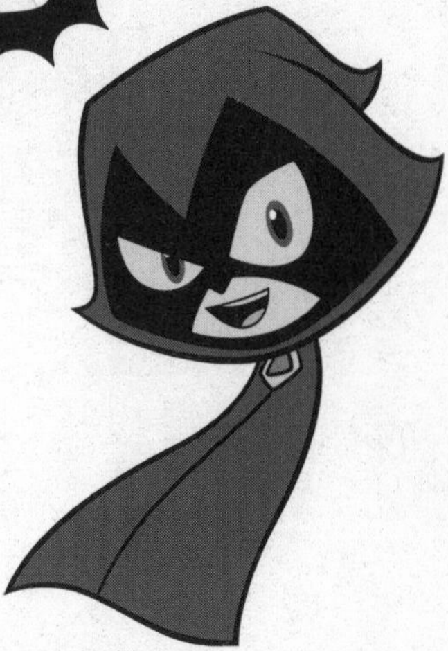

VIDEO GAME REFERENCES

IMAGINATION

©1984

PUSH START BUTTON

IMAGINATION

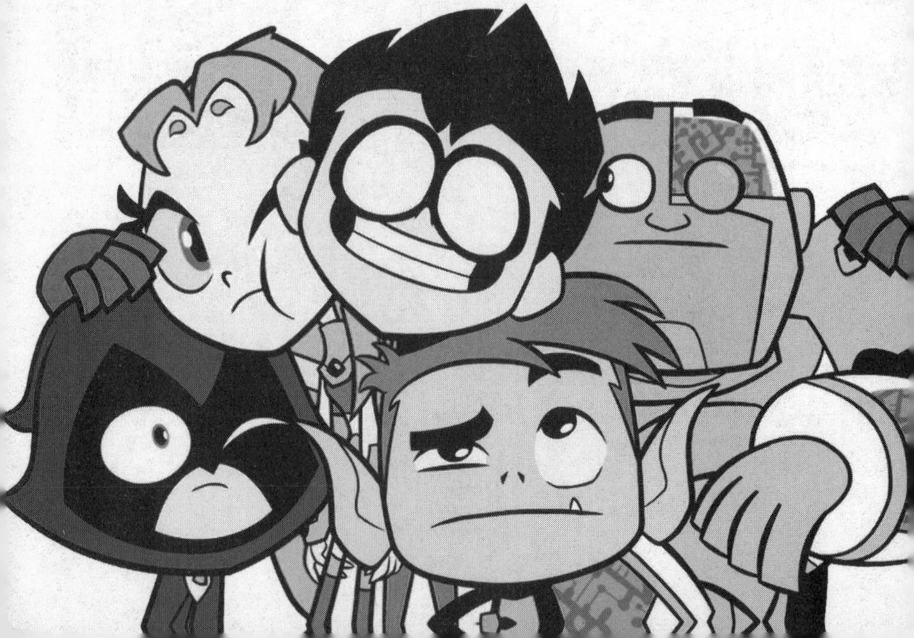

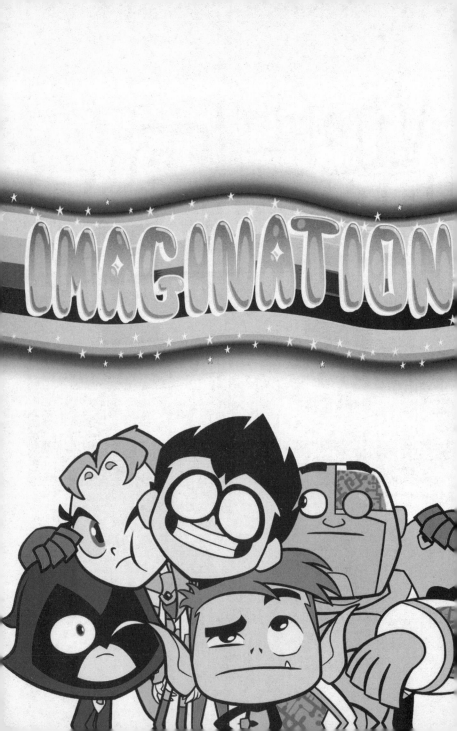

CHAPTER 1

"Titans! On the other side of this door lies a world of adventure…intrigue…and *danger*!" Robin announced loudly as he hopped from foot to foot in excitement. It was previously just an ordinary day in Titans Tower, the giant T-shaped skyscraper that stood at the edge of Jump City. Inside the building was assembled the world-famous team of junior crime fighters known as the Teen Titans.

Robin had gathered his fellow Teen Titans teammates together in the living room of the Tower. He was pointing to a closed door in excitement. Raven, Beast Boy, Starfire, and Cyborg sighed impatiently.

"Don't you ever get tired of being excited about *everything*?" asked Beast Boy.

"Yes, I *do*!" Robin said with excitement. "That's why I'm in therapy to lower my blood pressure! But this time I have reason to be excited, because I am about to show you something *truly* beyond your imagination!"

Starfire clasped her hands together and happily said, "*Ooooh*...imagination!"

Cyborg turned to Starfire. "And don't *you* ever get tired of saying '*Ooooh*' to everything Robin says?" he asked.

"Yes, I do!" she said. "I am only trying to be the polite!"

"And your pity does not go unnoticed, Star!" said Robin. "Now, as I was saying…"

Robin paused dramatically.

"Just open the door, Robin," Raven said, not bothering to keep the annoyance out of her voice.

"Fine," said Robin with a frown.

He waved his hands with a flourish, turned the doorknob, and opened the door.

"Behold!" he said grandly. "The wonders of *imagination*!"

The Titans walked through the doorway and entered a room. They looked around and shrugged.

"It's just an empty room," observed Cyborg.

"Until we *fill it*!" urged Robin.

"Yeah, that's how rooms work," said Raven. "They're empty until you fill them."

"But we're going to fill it with…*imagination*!" Robin yelled, letting his excitement get the better of him.

Starfire sighed and said, "*Ooooh*…imagination," this time with a bit less enthusiasm.

"Thank you, Star!" said Robin. "Your *ooooh*s are the fuel that keeps me going!"

Robin turned to his teammates and said, "We are standing in a state-of-the-art virtual-reality room that can simulate any environment *imaginable*—"

"Okay, that *is* cool!" interrupted Cyborg.

"—*for training purposes*!" concluded Robin.

The other Titans groaned at the mention of the word *training*.

6

"*Training?* Don't you ever get tired of making cool things boring?" asked Raven.

"Yes, I do!" Robin said enthusiastically. "And I'm in therapy for *that* as well!"

Beast Boy looked surprised and asked, "How many therapists do you have, bro?"

Robin glared at Beast Boy and muttered, "That's between me and my therapists!"

Robin faced his teammates again and said, "Now watch as cutting-edge technology transforms this empty room into a world of…"

He paused dramatically, waiting for his teammates to finish his sentence.

Together, and without much enthusiasm, they all muttered, "…imagination."

"That's right—*imagination*!" Robin said as he removed a square plastic cartridge from his Utility Belt. A large "Copyright 1984" notice could be seen on top of the cartridge.

Robin walked over to a control panel on a wall and inserted the cartridge into a slot on the panel. He waited a few seconds. And then he waited a few seconds more.

As the other Titans sighed, Robin removed the cartridge and blew on it. A thick layer of dust wafted off the cartridge. He inserted it into the control panel again.

BOOP! CHUNKA! BOOP! CHUNKA! BOOP!

Suddenly, the room was filled with the sound of tinny, synthesized notes emitted

from an electronic keyboard. Dozens of
red and green lasers shot out of the control
panel. The Titans looked around in shock to
see that they had all been transformed into
video-game characters. But they were not
sleek, gleaming high-definition video-game
characters with smoothly colored rendering.
They had been transformed into chunky,
flat-colored characters with rough, uneven,
and pixilated edges where they used to be
rounded.

Cyborg examined his newly chunky hands and said, "Uh, I thought you said that this was cutting-edge?"

Raven glared at her rough edges and said, "Yeah. These graphics are terrible. We look like characters from a 1980s video game."

"They're not terrible," Robin said angrily. "It's a world of *imagination*!"

Starfire opened her mouth—with its freshly square-edged lips—and said sadly, "*Ooooooooooooooh*…imagination!"

As her other teammates glared at her, she quietly explained, "I am just attempting to calm Robin."

"That's what my *therapy* is for!" snapped Robin.

"Wait. Are you sure this is a virtual-reality

10

machine and not some retro video game?" asked Cyborg.

"It's a high-tech battle simulator I bought at the swap meet!" shouted Robin. "And they don't sell junk at the swap meet!"

Robin took a moment to calm himself and then continued. "I've set up five different simulated missions to test each of us individually. Now, Titans, are you ready to experience a world of imagination?!"

"Not really," admitted Cyborg.

"Nope," added Raven.

"Do we *have* to?" asked Beast Boy.

Starfire yawned and muttered, "*Oooooh*… imagination."

"*Love* that patronizing attitude, Star!" said Robin. "You're up first!"

Robin removed a remote-control device from his Utility Belt and pushed a button on it. Starfire disappeared from the room.

CHAPTER 2

Blocky video-game character Starfire found herself standing on the edge of a grassy cliff, surrounded by badly colored rocks. Water fell unconvincingly from a nearby waterfall.

"Oh, this battle simulation looks like the beginning of a great quest of legend!" Starfire said happily.

Suddenly, with a fanfare of tinny, synthesized trumpets, a box filled with ragged letters

13

appeared above Starfire. It read, "Starfire's Quest: The Legend of the Legendary Quest."

With jerky movements, Starfire flew through the air, approached a nearby cave, and entered.

Inside the cave, Starfire discovered another video-game character. It was an old man. He had a long white beard and was wearing a brown robe. Next to him were two metal urns crackling with poorly colored yellow-and-red flames.

The old man held up a brown sword that looked more like a brown stick and said, "It's dangerous to go alone. Take this."

"Thank you," Starfire said politely, "but I will be fine without the stick."

"But you are alone!" protested the man. "And it's dangerous to go alone!"

14

"Are you not also alone?" asked Starfire.

The man paused to consider this and said, "It's…well, yes. I guess it has been some time since I have talked to anyone. My wife used to visit before she left me. That was years ago."

"Um…" said Starfire as she turned to walk away.

"I'm very lonely," offered the man.

"I…should continue my quest," said Starfire as she moved toward the entrance to the cave.

"Yes, of course," he continued sadly. "Don't mind this old

man! You're young. You have things to do. I'll just be here, sad and alone, with the wooden sword that no one wants."

"I suppose you *could* come with me," Starfire said doubtfully.

The man brightened and said, "You mean...leave the cave?"

"Yes!" said Starfire. "Join me in the quest of legend, sad old man!"

"Hot dog!" said the man as he jumped jerkily up and down. "I'll bring the sword!"

"A wooden sword is useless, but *wonderful*!" Starfire said with a smile.

BOOP! CHUNKA! BOOP! CHUNKA! BOOP!

Together, to the thumping sounds of a synthesized keyboard, Starfire and the old man left the cave and wandered into a nearby forest. They soon came upon four aqua-colored squid monsters that looked like large mushrooms. The man hoisted his wooden sword as the squids scuttled toward them.

"Be careful, hero! These are dangerous creatures!" cried the man.

He swatted at one of the squids with the wooden sword, but the squid quickly spat a layer of thick, inky, black goo onto the old man's head.

"Ouch! Protect me from this vicious beast, hero!" cried the man as he ran to hide behind Starfire.

"This beast is not vicious, sad old man!" said Starfire. "He merely desires the scratchy scratchies."

Starfire reached out her blocky hand to rub the side of one squid monster. The squid smiled. She then moved to touch the other three monsters. As she caressed the monsters, she sang, *"Scratchy scratchy scratchy scratch all the livelong days and months!"*

Starfire and the four squid monsters and the old man all did a happy dance together.

After the dance, Starfire turned to one of the squid monsters and asked, "Squid monster, will you join us on our quest of legend?"

The squid monster squirted some ink in reply and happily joined Starfire and the old man on their quest.

BOOP! CHUNKA! BOOP! CHUNKA! BOOP!

A graphic appeared above Starfire that read, "Squid monster has joined your party."

"Joy!" said Starfire as the three of them walked to a nearby village. There they discovered a distressed woman running after a chicken.

"Hero! Please help!" the woman called out. "My cooccalaka has escaped!"

"You mean the chicken?" asked Starfire.

"No, *cooccalaka*!" insisted the woman.

The old man stepped forward and brandished his sword.

"I'll handle this," he said as he waved the wooden sword at the chicken.

This seemed to enrage the chicken, which immediately began pecking at the old man.

"Oh, the pain!" cried the man. "Ow, my eyes! Help!"

After the chicken finished attacking the old man, it scampered off.

"Please, hero," the woman said to Starfire as she held aloft a glass bottle. "Catch my cooccalaka, and I'll reward you with this empty bottle!"

"That is the useless reward," observed Starfire as she chased after the chicken.

She soon caught the bird and returned it to the woman.

A graphic appeared above Starfire that read, "Cooccalaka has joined your party."

BOOP! CHUNKA! BOOP! CHUNKA! BOOP!

Starfire did a new happy dance with the

chicken, the woman, the old man, and the squid monster.

"You are gathering an *army*," said the old man. "You are truly the hero of legend! You will slay the villain for *sure*!"

"Slay?" said Starfire. "Oh, but I just wish to *dance*!"

The old man shrugged and said, "Works for me!"

BOOP! CHUNKA! BOOP! CHUNKA! BOOP!

And so they danced.

Just then, interrupting the dance party, a graphic appeared above Starfire that read, "While you were dancing, the evil wizard has taken over the world. All is in ruins. Game over!"

ZERRPPP!

CHAPTER 3

Jagged video-game Beast Boy looked around as he stood at the edge of a four-lane highway.

"Wonder what my battle training is," he pondered. "Fight an army? Save the princess? Ninja adventure?"

Suddenly, a series of words scrolled above him. They read, "Cross the Street. Copyright 1981. Press Start."

"Cross the *street*?" he said with indignation.

"C'mon! Why doesn't anyone think I can do anything *hard*?!"

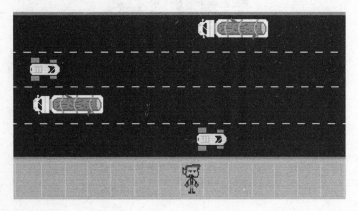

Beast Boy shook his head with disgust and faced the cars zooming along the busy road.

"Whatever," he said. "I'll just change into a li'l froggy frog and hop to the other side of the street."

Beast Boy transformed himself into a green frog and hopped onto the busy road.

SPLAT!

He was instantly flattened by a truck.

Beast Boy found himself at the edge of the road again.

"Okay, that guy totally came out of nowhere!" he complained as he hopped onto the road again.

SPLAT!

This time a taxicab ran over him.

"Who taught you how to *drive*?!" he yelled.

Froggy Beast Boy next tried to navigate a crosswalk.

SPLAT!

A car smashed into him in the middle of the crosswalk.

"I had the *right of way*!" he screamed.

Four more times Froggy Beast Boy tried to cross the road.

SPLAT! SPLAT! SPLAT! SPLAT!

And four more times he was run over.

"Why won't *anyone* stop for a frog?!" he yelled. "How am I supposed to cross this stupid road?!"

He paused to think for a moment and said, "*Cross the road.* Wait, that's it. This is a job for a *chicken*!"

Chuckling to himself, Beast Boy transformed himself into a green chicken and ran across the road.

CHOMP!

Chicken Beast Boy was swallowed whole by a hungry alligator that was waiting on the other side of the road.

As green chicken feathers floated through the air, a graphic appeared above the road that read, "Game over."

ZERRPPPP!

CHAPTER 4

Video-game character Raven—basically just a purplish cloak with eyes and a mouth in the middle—stared at the words above her that read, "Circle-Guy. Copyright 1978. Press Start." She was floating in a field of glowing yellow balls.

"So what's my big battle simulation?" she wondered aloud.

She glanced next to her and discovered

three other similarly dressed video-game characters that were hovering nearby. Each had a different-colored cloak: one red, one pink, and one violet.

"Look at us," Raven said. "We're dressed nice."

Just then, Raven noticed a large circular yellow creature chomping on the glowing balls.

"Hey, who's that Circle-Guy?" asked Raven.

"And why is he eating all the balls! We have to *stop* him!"

Raven charged after the circular creature, but her three companions just moved about randomly.

"You guys going to help or what?" Raven asked with annoyance.

The others just continued moving around aimlessly.

"Seriously, look at you guys! No wonder Circle-Guy just takes all your stuff!" Raven complained.

Suddenly, a pair of bright-red cherries appeared nearby.

CHOMP!

The yellow creature swallowed them whole.

"Hey, you guys!" called out Raven. "Look! Now he's eating your cherries! Come *on*!"

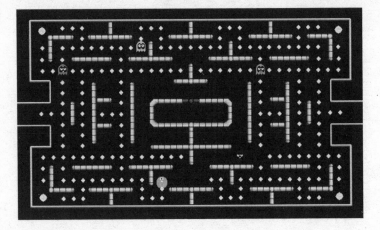

Raven floated closer to her companions.

"Now, let's focus," she said. "Move in form-ation on my command. Go!"

Raven and the trio of video game charac-ters floated aggressively toward the yellow creature.

CHOMP!

The circular creature swallowed an extra-big ball. Suddenly, the creature doubled in size. He charged toward Raven and her new friends in nice cloaks.

"I don't know what he ate, but it's making him *nuts!*" she yelled. "Pull back, pull back!"

CHOMP!

The circular creature ate Raven's pink companion.

"No!!!" cried Raven in dramatic anguish. "I'll never forget you, Pinky!"

She turned to glare at the circular creature and shouted, "Let's end this...*now!*"

Raven and her two remaining companions surrounded the circular creature. They moved closer and closer. The creature was caught like a rat in a trap!

Suddenly, a female circular creature arrived. She quickly swallowed Raven and her two friends.

CHOMP! CHOMP! CHOMP!

All that was physically left of Raven was a pair of floating eyes.

"*Owwwwwwwwwww!*" wailed Raven's weird floating eyes.

Her eyes then looked up and saw the words "Game over."

ZERRPPP!

CHAPTER 5

Video-game Cyborg was in the driver's seat of a car. He glanced up to see that the name of his game was "Pie Hunter."

"Booyah! Rev it up, baby," he yelled happily, practically bounching in his seat. "I *love* pie! This is gonna be so much *fuuuuuun*!"

Cyborg carefully checked his rearview mirror, adjusted

his seat belt, turned on the car engine, and carefully pulled onto the highway.

ZOOM!

Almost instantly, two cars sped around Cyborg, honking their horns at him.

"Slow down, you maniacs!" Cyborg yelled at the speeding cars. "Where did you learn to drive?"

HONK! HONK!

A car behind Cyborg started to tailgate him.

"I am going the posted speed limit!" Cyborg fumed. "Just go around! *Go around!*" He angrily tried to wave the other car past him.

Seconds later, the car sped by.

"Why is everybody in such a rush nowadays?" Cyborg fretted. "Driving is a privilege, not a right. Just enjoy the drive!"

He reached to turn on the radio and found some smooth jazz to relax his frazzled nerves. He was humming along happily until another car appeared behind him. It was an ominous-looking dark-purple vehicle, with a skull and crossbones painted on its hood.

"Oh, look at Tailgate Johnny back there," Cyborg said with a frown. He yelled at the other car, "You like my bumper stickers or what?!"

BLAM!

The other car pulled up next to Cyborg's car and then swerved to crash into it. Cyborg's car went skidding off the road and landed in a grassy field.

"Oh, great!" grumbled Cyborg as he climbed

out of his car. "*Just* what I need today!"

A man wearing sunglasses and a black suit jumped out of the other car and started running toward Cyborg.

"Now you're gonna *pay…*" the man said in a threatening tone of voice as he reached into his pocket.

"*What?!*" said Cyborg with indignation. "*You're* gonna pay, buddy! No way was that accident *my* fault. You better have insurance!"

The man in the dark suit looked confused. "Can we handle this without insurance?" he said. "I can't have another accident on my record."

"Well, you should have thought of that before you decided to drive so recklessly," lectured Cyborg.

36

"Come on," said the man. "I'll pay for the repairs in cash, okay?"

"Uh-uh, no way," said Cyborg.

"Ugh. Fine," said the man as he handed over his insurance card to Cyborg.

Minutes later, Cyborg was back on the road, humming happily to a smooth jazz tune again. He looked up to see a road sign.

"Oh, look at that!" he said. "Pie—next exit."

There were few things in the world that

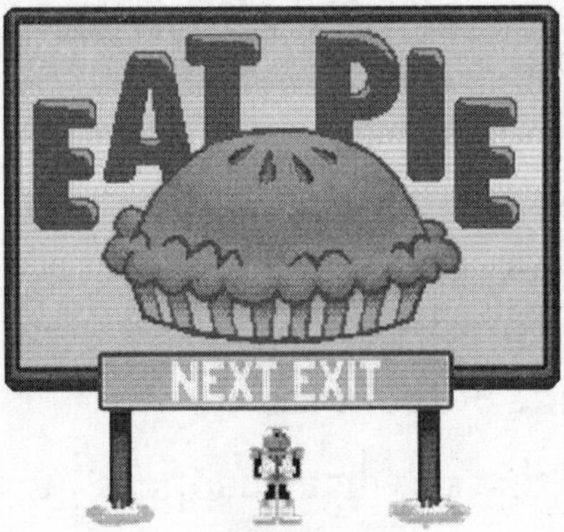
EAT PIE
NEXT EXIT

Cyborg loved as much as pie. He was about to start singing a song about pie when the sound of bullets filled the air. The purple car was behind him again, and this time the man was firing a gun.

"Oh my goodness!" yelled Cyborg. "This is so scary. I just wanted to get some pie!"

"You mess up my driving record; I mess up your face!" yelled the man in the purple car.

"You have the wrong person!" Cyborg screamed as he swerved to avoid the other car. "I am out for a responsible Sunday drive!"

"No pie for you!" chortled the man. "I make you die now!"

POW!

The purple car hit a pothole and skidded off the side of the road.

"And that's what happens to reckless

drivers," said Cyborg as he drove up to the pie shop. "And now it's time for pie!" he yelled as he happily got of out of his car.

WHAM! WHAM! WHAM!

Suddenly, a helicopter appeared above the pie shop. The man in the dark suit was flying the helicopter and firing a machine gun.

"I bet you did not know that I had a helicopter!" he called out as he fired at Cyborg's car.

BLAM!

A huge ball of fire erupted as Cyborg's car exploded.

"My *car*!" yelled Cyborg.

"I kill your stupid pies!" the man yelled as he fired at the pie shop.

KER-BLAM!

The pie shop went up in flames.

39

"Okay, I go now," the man said with a chuckle as he flew away.

Cyborg fell to the ground and moaned, "Oh, how I hate you, Pie Hunter. Is there *anything* more that can go wrong today?"

He glanced up to see the words "Game over."

ZERRPPP!

CHAPTER 6

Finally, it was time for Robin to face his video-game quest. A small, chunky hero, he stood atop a stone castle nestled at the foot of a mighty green mountain range. His game title scrolled brightly across the sky: "Save the Princess, Bro."

"The perfect battle simulation requires the perfect mission," Robin said confidently. "I'm coming for you, Princess!"

His blocky cape flowing behind him, Robin jumped from a tower of the castle and ran along a stone wall. A snail-like creature was scuttling toward him. Robin bravely ran forward.

"Hope you like pancakes because that's what I'm serving for breakfast!" Robin yelled as he landed on top of the creature. "Foot stomp!" he called out as he flattened the aggreessive thing underneath him.

Just for fun, he turned around and jumped on the creature two more times. "Foot stomp! Foot stomp!"

Robin looked up and noticed a glowing box floating above him. There was an exclamation mark painted on the side of the box. "I bet there's something good in there," he said, using his detective skills.

Robin crouched down and then jumped up, hitting his head on the box. "Ow!" he said as paper money popped out of the box.

Robin jumped up to hit his head on the box again. And again. More money floated down from the box. "Ow! Ow! This hurts," he pouted as he gathered the money. "But I've got to get this money…all this sweet, sweet money."

Six jumps later, Robin was feeling a bit dizzy. "Ow! Money! OW! I'm rich! Ha-ha! Ow! *That's* a concussion! But I'm rich! Ow!"

Robin glanced around and noticed a large

metal pipe extending from the top of a castle tower. "No more distractions," he said as he ran over to the edge of the metal pipe. "I'm coming, Princess! I wonder where this large pipe goes?" He peered into the dark pipe. "Well, only one way to find out!"

With than, Robin jumped into the pipe.

"Oh, man! That stinks!" Robin yelled as he plummeted down the pipe. "Why did I just go down a *sewage pipe*?! This is so *gross*! So much *sewage* in this *sewage pipe*!"

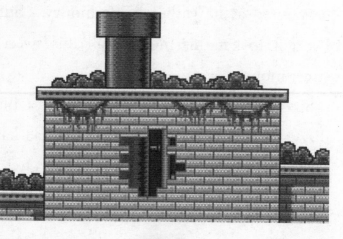

SPLAT!

Robin emerged from the bottom of the sewage pipe and landed with a thud on the sticky floor of a dungeon. He was covered in sewage.

"It's dark in this dungeon," said Robin. "I can barely read those words on the wall. What do they say?"

He wiped the sewage from his eyes and managed to decipher these words: "Game over. Continue? Yes/No."

Robin reached a sticky finger forward and chose "No." This whole training simulation thing had gotten way out of hand, his head hurt, and he was covered in sewage. He was done.

ZERRRRPPPPPP!

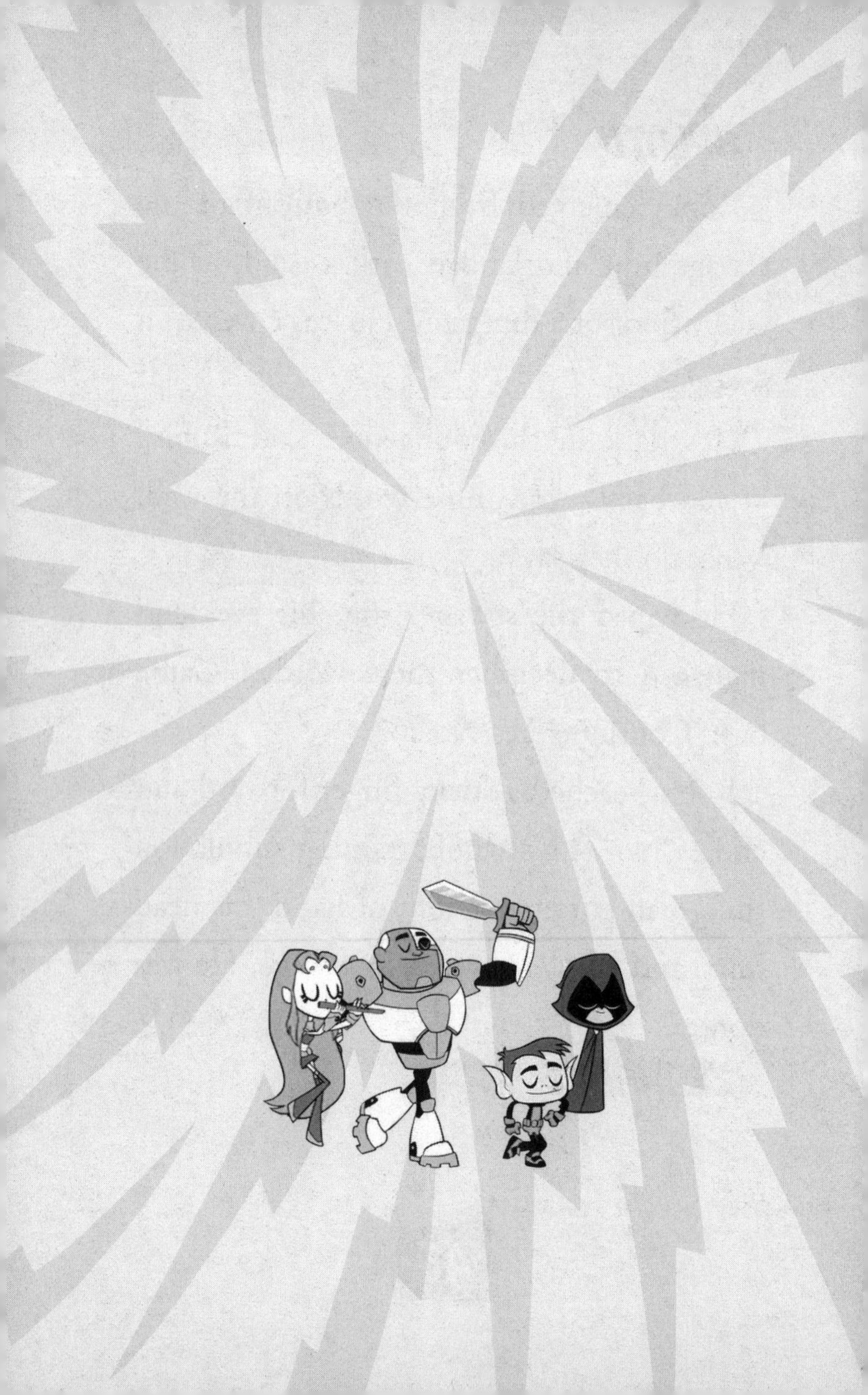

RIDE THE DRAGON

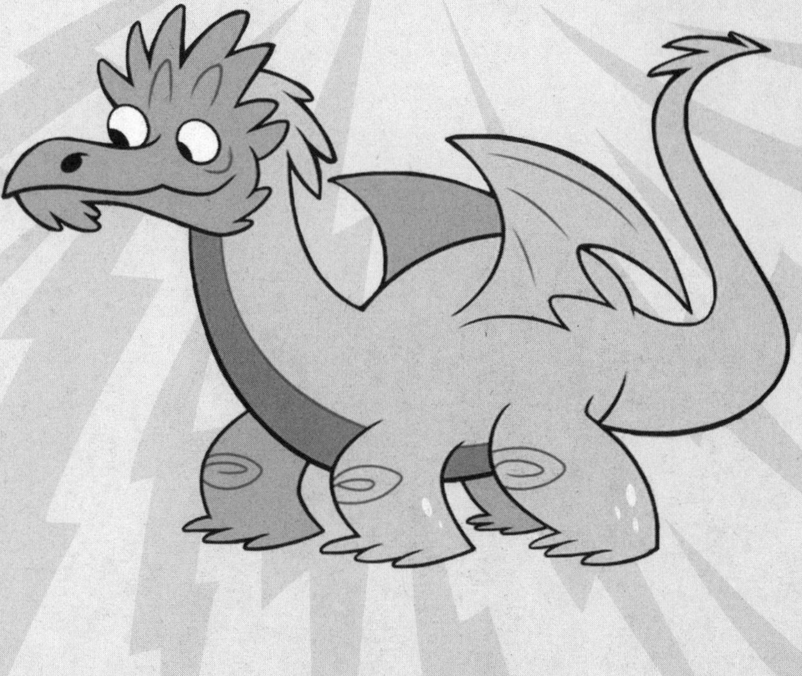

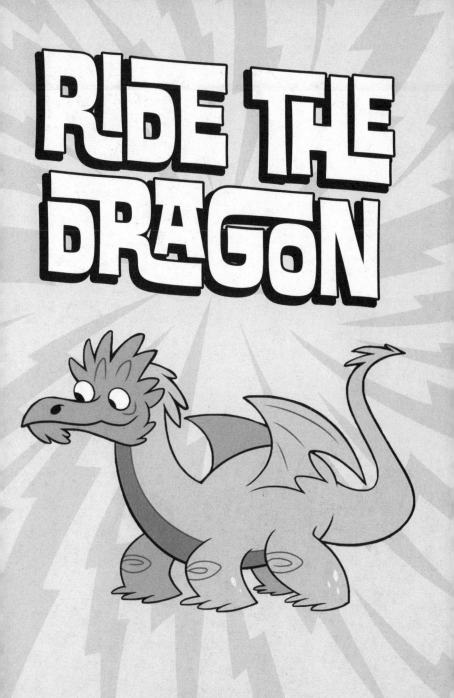

CHAPTER 1

It was nighttime in a dark and ominous forest.
Four of the Teen Titans—Cyborg, Raven,
Starfire, and Beast Boy—were making their
way down a wooded path. They were studying
the ground carefully, searching for tracks.

ROAAAAAR!

A monstrous red dragon suddenly appeared
in front of them. It had blazing yellow eyes
and a mouth full of razor-sharp teeth. As the

Titans jumped out of the way, the dragon shot a blast of red-hot flames out of its mouth.

"The dragon!" called out Cyborg. "We found it!"

Beast Boy turned to his teammates and asked, "So what's the plan?"

Cyborg frowned and narrowed his eyes. "There can only be one plan...." he announced seriously as he removed a sword from his armored suit.

The others leaned forward to hear his plan.

A smile filled Cyborg's face as he jumped up and down. "I wanna ride that dragon!" he said happily.

Beast Boy laughed and said, "Awesome! Ride that dragon, yo!"

Cyborg took a leap and jumped onto the dragon's back. The dragon smiled in response

and waved its spiky tail as Cyborg got settled.
"*Ohhh!* I am riding this dragon!" he yelled.

"I, too, wish to ride the dragon!" Starfire
said.

Cyborg leaned down and said, "Then come
on and ride the dragon!"

Starfire flew through the air and landed on
the back of the dragon. "Now *I* am riding the
dragon!" she said with a smile.

"You two!" Cyborg called out to his other teammates. "Come ride this dragon!"

Beast Boy and Raven jumped onto the dragon, which spread its wings and started dancing in the forest.

"We're all riding the dragon!" yelled the happy heroes.

Suddenly, the voice of Robin cut through the merrymaking.

"Whoa-whoa-whoa! What is going on here?!" he demanded.

POOF!

Instantly, the dragon disappeared, and the Teen Titans found themselves perched on top of the couch in the middle of the Titans Tower living room. The ride atop the dragon was unfortunately just a part of a fantasy board game. The open cardboard box for the game was on the floor.

"We're playing this awesome game called 'Dragon's Fire!'" said Cyborg as he picked up the box and showed it to Robin.

"It's really cool," said Raven. "We pretend to ride a dragon."

Starfire smiled and said, "You should ride the dragon with us!"

"I'd love to…" Robin began quietly. Then he started yelling angrily, "…except you are playing it *completely wrong*! This game has a strict set of rules that *must* be followed!"

"Rules?" asked Beast Boy. "We don't care about rules, we just want to get lost in the magic of a fantasy world, yo!"

"But if you follow the rules you'll experience a magical, fantastical adventure that will leave you *frothing* with joy!" argued Robin.

"I wish to do the joy froth!" said Starfire.

"Then let's get magical, bro!" agreed Cyborg.

"All right!" said Robin as he reached into the box and removed a thick rule book, a pile of papers, and the playing board. He opened up the board in front of his teammates and placed it on top of the coffee table.

"The first step on your magical adventure is to fill out these *worksheets*," he said as he distributed a pile of papers to each Titan.

Raven asked suspiciously, "What is this, homework?"

"Homework?" scoffed Robin. "Ha! *Bo-ring!*
This is a worksheet to calculate your character's skills using basic mathematics!"

"Man, c'mon, you know our brains can't
do math-magics," argued Beast Boy.

Robin sighed in frustration and then said,
"Fine. Then just draw a picture of your
character and I'll do the rest."

"That we can do!" said Cyborg as he started scribbling on his worksheet.

Minutes later, the Titans proudly held up their drawings.

"Check it, I'm a hyena!" said Beast Boy.

"I'm a horrible monster hiding under a cloak," said Raven.

"I am the warrior princess!" said Starfire.

"And I'm the Tin Man, baby," said Cyborg. *"Clankity clank!"*

"And what is your character, Robin?" asked Starfire.

"Oh, me? No big deal," Robin said with some fake modesty. "Just a half-elf battle-mage called Nightshadow! Savior of the nine kingdoms of men, Nightshadow wields not only the Magical Staff of Gimesh but also the Sacred Flute of Katang!"

Cyborg was impressed. "You got a stick *and* a flute?" he said. "Nice!"

"Thank you," replied Robin. "Now, I've crafted a magical adventure that involves some *pretty exciting stuff*!"

"Riding dragons?" asked a clearly excited Cyborg.

"No!" said Robin.

"Necromancers?" asked Raven.

"Nope!"

"The fairies?" asked Starfire.

"Even *better*!" said Robin. "We will embark upon a quest to retrieve a key."

Beast Boy smiled and asked, "A magical key?"

"A regular key," said Robin.

"That opens a magic door?" Cyborg asked happily.

"A regular door!"

Raven frowned and said, "Robin, that sounds boring."

"I *knew* you'd be excited!" Robin said quickly. "Let's get started!" he continued. "Our party travels upon the southern road toward Valaheim, through the ancient forest of Threllegh'Vhehn."

"Thrilla-what?" asked Cyborg.

"Threllegh'Vhehn."

"Tralling-vhahaga?" offered Beast Boy.

"The *forest*!" Robin said with frustration. "Your party is in the *forest*!"

Beast Boy jumped up and said, "A forest huh? I wanna climb some trees!"

Robin nodded in agreement and held out some bright-red multi-sided dice.

"Okay. Roll the dice," he said.

"No, bro," argued Beast Boy. "I said I want to *climb trees*."

"I heard you," said Robin. "In this game, these dice determine your every action. If you want to climb a tree, you have to roll the dice."

"Ugh, fine," grumbled Beast Boy as he reached for the dice. "Gimme."

Beast Boy rolled one of the dice. It landed with the number one showing on top.

"A one!" Beast Boy said with excitement. "That's good, right? I'm number one!"

"No, that is the *worst* number," said Robin as he read from the rule book. "Hyena falls from the tree, hits his head on a branch, and gets a concussion."

"Aw, c'mon," said Beast Boy with disappointment.

"I wish to search for fairies!" said Starfire as she reached for the dice.

She rolled and also landed a one.

Robin read from the book, "The warrior princess attempts to search for fairies, but hits her head on a branch and gets a concussion."

"Sadness," said Starfire.

"Yeah, this is boring," said Raven.

"It's magical!" argued Robin.

"Then why do you keep killing the magic

60

with all this *boring* stuff?" asked Cyborg.

"I told you, the game has a *strict set of rules!*" Robin yelled angrily. *"You're ruining everything!"*

THUMP! THUMP! THUMP!

With each word, Robin pounded his fist on top of the board game for emphasis. The other Titans jumped back in surprise.

VOOOOOOOOOOOM!

Suddenly, the board game started to shake and emit a loud humming noise. Then, it exploded with a dazzling array of white sparks.

"What is the happening?!" asked Starfire with panic in her voice.

WHOOOOOSH!

As the five Titans yelled out in surprise, they were all tossed into the air and then magically sucked into the land of Dragon's Fire!

CHAPTER

"Aaaaaaah!" yelled the Titans as they tumbled through the air and landed with a **THUD** on the floor of a forest. Glowing red mountains surrounded them, and there was a dark castle in the distance.

"Whoa! Check it out!" Beast Boy said as he caught a glimpse of himself in a pool of water. He had transformed into a giant, fuzzy, green hyena-like creature.

"I have become the warrior princess of my dreams!" said Starfire as she raised her armor-clad arm and displayed a gleaming sword in her hand.

Raven, who had grown twice as large, said with a chuckle, "Just call me a horrible monster hiding under a cloak."

"And I'm the Tin Man, baby," said an enlarged Cyborg, hoisting a giant metal war hammer. *"Clankity clank! Clankity clank!"*

Robin frowned and noticed that he had not grown at all. His only noticeable changes were a small cloth cap that covered his hair and a wooden staff that he held in his hands. "I thought Nightshadow would be a little taller than this," he grumbled.

As the Titans started walking through the dark forest, Beast Boy said, "Yo, I think we's in that forest of Tralla-vahahaga!"

"Threllegh'Vhehn," corrected Robin.

"Throohoolo-volooohoo," offered Starfire.

"Threllegh'Vhehn," said Robin through gritted teeth.

"Thruhupvruhup?" asked Raven.

"Threllegh'Vhehn!" shouted Robin.

"Oh, you mean Trooppadoopadoop," said Cyborg.

"Just call it *the forest*!" screamed Robin. "And obviously, we're now stuck in here because *you* didn't follow the rules of the game!"

"So when you said the game was magical you meant, like, *for real*?" asked Raven.

"Of course! It's all about wizards and dragons, what did you expect?"

Cyborg smiled and said, "This is actually pretty cool. We could see a dragon *for real*!"

Starfire gasped with happiness and said, "We could *ride* the dragon for the reals!"

"I could climb these trees for reals!" said Beast Boy as he clasped his fuzzy paws around a tree trunk.

Robin pulled Beast Boy away from the tree and said, "*Absolutely not!* That's the kind of imaginative excitement that got us into this

 mess. The only way out is to finish the original adventure and find the key! *Follow me,*

follow the rules! Understand?"

"Okay…fine," the other Titans grumbled and reluctantly agreed.

"Great," said Robin. "We'll start where all great adventures start.…"

Robin led the Titans to the edge of the forest, and then he pointed his wooden staff dramatically toward a small brick building in an advanced state of disrepair. The wooden beams holding up the roof were filled with termite holes, and a smell of rancid cooking oil wafted from the cracked windows. A sign outside the building advertised it as the INN OF THE BULLIED BONES.

Cyborg frowned and said, "What kind of great adventure starts at a greasy motel?"

"Not at all," corrected Robin as he pushed open the decaying wooden door and led the

Titans into the building. "It's a charming inn!"

The Titans blinked as they beheld the interior of the inn. The walls of the large single room were decorated with skulls and other bones; only a few sputtering candles illuminated the gloom. Sitting at wooden tables were a half dozen goblins, trolls, and orcs.

"Good morrow, my lords and gentlefolk," Robin said with a bow.

The creatures in the inn glared at him. One of the orcs burped.

At the end of the room, a green goblin innkeeper stood behind a counter. He scowled and spat on a cracked goblet to clean it.

"*Oooh*, look!" said Robin with excitement. "A grizzled old innkeeper like that is sure to point us in the direction of adventure!"

The goblin innkeeper spat on the counter and used his tongue to wipe it.

"Ew," said Raven.

Robin boldly walked up to the counter and said, "Hark, innkeep! Have you any work for a band of brave adventurers?"

"Aye," the goblin said with a raspy voice. "I've got a problem."

He then spat into a skull on top of the counter.

"There are vicious creatures in the basement," he continued. "Claws...red eyes...fangs like you've never seen!"

The Titans' eyes widened with excitement.

"Dragons?!" they asked hopefully.

The innkeeper spat and said, "Rats."

The Titans groaned with disappointment.

"So call an exterminator," suggested Cyborg.

Starfire turned to walk out of the inn. "Now let us find the real adventure!" she said to her teammates.

"Not so fast!" called out Robin. "Remember, to get home we have to finish *this* adventure!"

"Fine," said Beast Boy grudgingly. "But we wanna see something magical, bro."

"Oh, you'll see something *magical* all right..." promised Robin as he pulled open the door.

The Titans slowly made their way down the stone steps that led to the basement. Robin was in the lead.

"Steady yourselves..." he said as he raised

a candle and stepped onto the sticky floor of the basement.

"I got this," said Beast Boy as he moved forward. "Rats are my bros."

ROAAAAR!

Suddenly, three giant rats emerged from the shadows and started snarling at the Titans. The sharp fangs of the giant rats glowed in the candlelight.

"*Eeeeeek!*" screamed the Titans as they quickly jumped back.

"*Aaah!* They're not bros!" yelled Beast Boy.

"I *told* you we'd see something magical!" Robin said brightly. "Look at the size of those rats! To arms, friends!"

Cyborg raised his war hammer and cried out, "Prepare to taste the Tin Man's war hammer! *Rahhh!*"

Suddenly, Cyborg was unable to move. His hammer hovered in the air above him.

"I…I can't attack them!" he yelled. "Something is holding me back."

Robin sighed and held out a multi-sided die.

"Of course you can't," said Robin. "You have to roll the dice to attack."

72

"*Really?*" Cyborg asked with a frustrated sigh. "Fine…"

Cyborg rolled the die on the basement floor. It showed a one. "Another *one*?!" he yelled. "This die is broken!"

Cyborg was able to swing his war hammer, but it didn't come anywhere near the rats.

"Now the rats get to roll," said Robin.

One of the rats reached forward to roll the die. It landed with a ten. The rats smiled.

"*Hmm.* A ten," observed Robin. "Not bad."

"What does a ten get…?" began Cyborg.

Before he could finish his sentence, the three rats jumped through the air and landed on top of Cyborg.

BLAM! BLAM! BLAM!

"Ow! Ow! Rats everywhere!" Cyborg cried out as the rats pummeled and pounded him.

"Gimme that!" said Raven as she grabbed the die and quickly rolled it. She rolled a fifteen.

"Nice!" she said. "Let's try a magic spell: *Azarath Metrion Zinthos!*"

Thanks to Raven's spell, the rats suddenly stopped attacking Cyborg. They looked around in confusion for a few seconds.

"Phew…" said Cyborg with relief.

BLAM! BLAM! BLAM!

The rats then resumed their attacks on Cyborg.

"Did Raven not cast her spell?" Starfire asked with confusion.

"Yes. And it *worked*!" said Robin with satisfaction. "Didn't you see how the rats were distracted for a moment?"

Raven frowned and said, "Wait, I cast a *distraction spell*?!"

"You're only *level one*," explained Robin as

he held Raven's worksheet in his hand. "So that's your best spell."

Raven shook her head in disgust and said, "Now your rules are taking the magic out of magic!"

BLAM! BLAM! BLAM!

The rats continued to attack Cyborg.

"Make them stop!" Cyborg pleaded. "Ow! Ow!"

"Give me that worksheet," said Raven as she yanked the paper from Robin's hand. She

quickly changed her level from "one" to "one
hundred."

"*Azarath Metrion Zinthos!*" she chanted.

With a magical blast of energy, the rats
exploded into tiny puffs of dust.

"Phew…" said the battered Cyborg.

"Changing your power level was against
the rules of the game!" shouted Robin as he
waved his wooden staff in the air.

"And yet it worked!" observed Starfire.

Robin grumbled as he walked away. "I don't
believe this. People making up rules, messing
up everything…"

Suddenly, he stopped in front of two large wooden doors.

"Oh, look!" he said. "There appears to be a secret passage behind these two doors where the rats came from!"

He turned to the Titans and said, "Exciting! Are you guys feeling it? The adventure? Who knows what awaits us beyond this door?"

"Who would have thought fantasy could be so un-fantastic?" asked Raven.

"*Shhh,*" said Robin as he slowly began to

open one of the doors. Beyond the door they could see a dark room.

"Perhaps the fairy party awaits within," said Starfire with a smile.

"Oh, sick!" said Beast Boy. "All dancing with mermaids and—"

"Stop imagining things!" yelled Robin. "Mermaids and fairies are not going to help us complete this adventure. Now, stand ready!"

The Titans held their breath as they slowly filed into the next room. When their eyes adjusted to the gloom, they all gasped with shock!

CHAPTER 3

A large red dragon was curled up in a ball, sleeping on the floor of the room.

All of the Titans but Robin jumped up and down with delight and yelled happily, "A dragon!"

"*Shhhh!*" Robin whispered angrily. "If this dragon wakes up, it will *eat our heads*! Now follow me. Quietly."

He pointed to a stone pedestal on the other

side of the room. A shiny brass key had been placed on top of the pedestal.

"The key to getting us out of here is in sight," said Robin.

Robin started moving carefully past the dragon, walking as quietly as possible.

"We're almost clear...." whispered Robin.

He turned back to see Beast Boy climbing onto the dragon's leg.

"What are you *doing*?!" Robin said in a strangled whisper.

"We wanna ride the dragon!" explained Beast Boy.

"Just for one tiny minute!" said Starfire as she climbed up the dragon's tail.

"Absolutely not!" said Robin through gritted teeth.

"Bro, that is an actual dragon that we could be riding right now," argued Cyborg.

"Yeah, you said this world was full of magic," said Beast Boy. "But we ain't done nothing but roll dice and fight rats!"

"*That's the game!*" shouted Robin. "And we could be doing that from the *comfort of our couch*…but *no*! You had to use your dumb imaginations! And look where that got us!"

BAM! BAM! BAM!

With his last words, Robin angrily slammed his wooden staff against the floor.

The noise awakened the dragon, who quickly opened his yellow eyes to glare at the

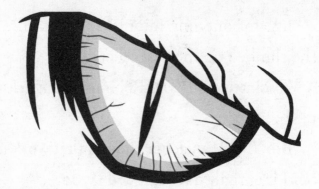

Titans. His mouth opened wide, and bright red flames shot out.

"Eeeeek!" screamed the Titans, scrambling to get out of the way.

The dragon shifted his giant head toward Robin and spoke in a deep, rumbling voice.

"You blame *them* for being trapped here?" the dragon asked Robin.

"Uh, yeah," Robin said angrily. "They broke the rules!"

"Ha! Young elf, it was you who caused this!" said the dragon. "You were brought here for ruining this magical game!"

"What?!" cried Robin.

The other Titans pointed at Robin and started to laugh.

"Oh, in the face," said Starfire with a giggle.

"Imagination is true magic and has no rules!" rumbled the dragon. "It's so simple, I can't believe you don't know that."

As Robin folded his arms over his chest and started to sulk, Cyborg took a running leap and jumped up onto the dragon's back.

"I wanna ride the dragon!" Cyborg called out.

Moments later, he was joined by Beast Boy, Raven, and Starfire. They were all perched on top of the dragon's back.

"*We're riding the dragon!*" they sang together.

Cyborg leaned over to call out to Robin.

"Come ride the dragon with us, bro!" said Cyborg.

"Yes, young elf," urged the dragon. "Come and ride me!"

"Well, I guess I *could* give it a try," said Robin as he jumped up onto the dragon. A smile filled Robin's face.

"I'm riding the dragon and it's *fun*!" bellowed Robin.

"Delightful! Delightful!" called out the dragon as he leapt into the air.

The Titans held tight to the dragon's back as he soared even higher.

"This is true magic and fantasy!" said the dragon. "Congratulations, you've discovered that imagination was the key to your escape all along!"

The Titans happily high-fived one another.

"And now…" announced the dragon, "you die."

"Awesome!" yelled Beast Boy, and then he said, "Wait…*what?*"

WHOOOOOOOSH!

A fireball of bright red-and-yellow flames shot out of the dragon's mouth and incinerated the Teen Titans.

CHAPTER 4

Back at Titans Tower, smoke gently drifted up from five tiny piles of black ash on the couch.

Game time was officially over.

For now.

And probably no more riding the dragon going forward.

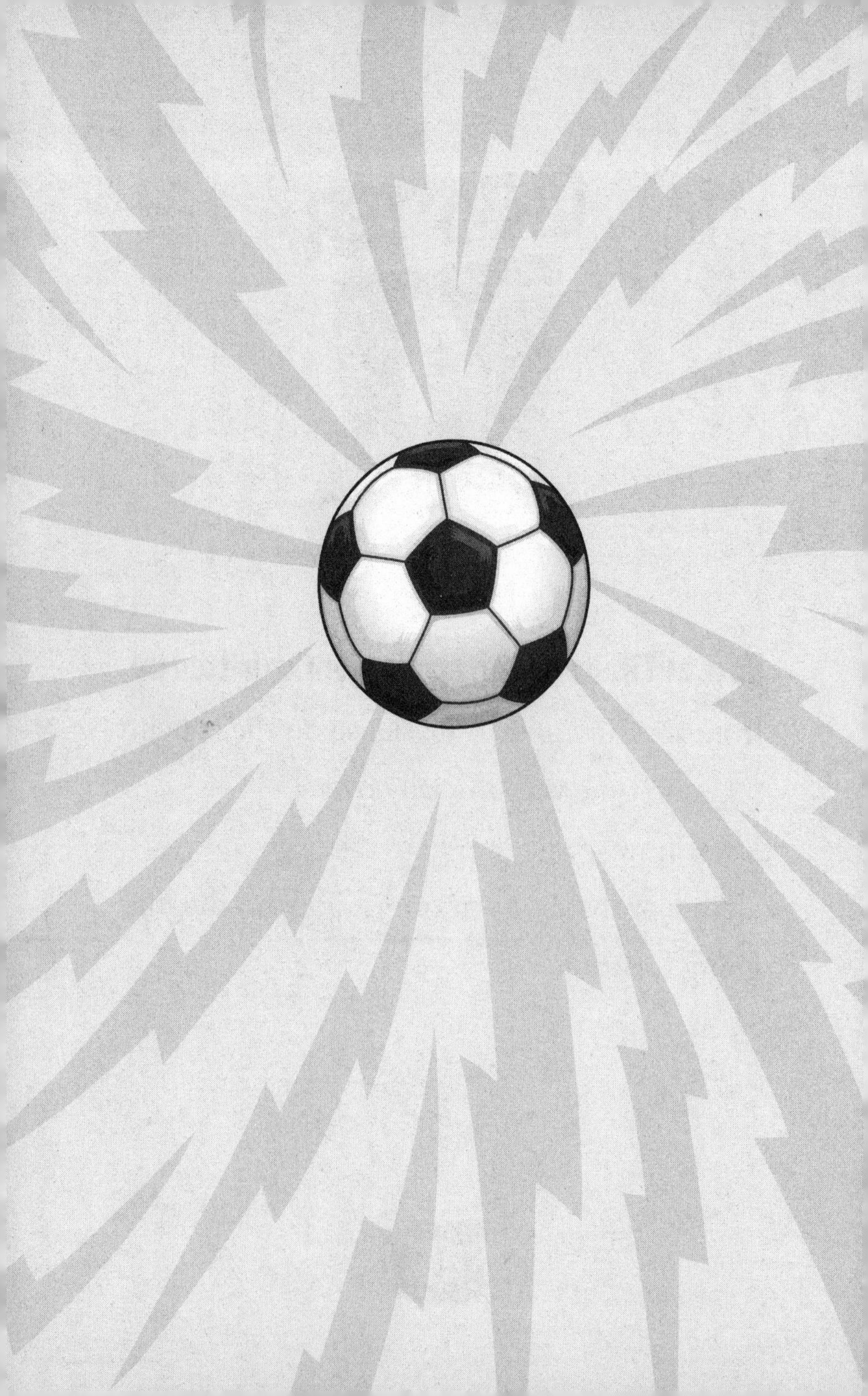

KICKING A BALL AND PRETENDING TO BE HURT

CHAPTER

Today, four of the legendary Teen Titans— Cyborg, Raven, Starfire, and Beast Boy— were lounging in the living room. They were sprawled on the couch and watching TV. Looks of boredom filled their faces as Cyborg clicked the remote every few seconds to change channels.

Suddenly, a small, brightly colored metal

canister came flying into the middle of the living room.

BOOM!

The canister exploded and filled the room with dark-gray smoke.

The four Titans coughed and frantically waved their hands to clear the smoke from the room. When enough of the smoke had disappeared, they discovered Robin standing in the middle of the room. Naturally, he had

exploded the canister just to make a dramatic entrance.

"Dude, your dramatic entrances are bad for my lungs!" complained Beast Boy.

Robin ignored Beast Boy and faced his teammates with excitement.

"Titans!" Robin shouted. "As you all know, today is Sports Day!"

Raven muttered, "I didn't know that."

Robin glared at Raven for a second and then said, "Well, then as you all know—*except for Raven*—today is Sports Day!"

Beast Boy shrugged and said, "I didn't know either, bro."

Robin spun around to face Cyborg and Starfire.

"Well, *you two* know that it's Sports Day, right?" he asked.

"Nope," said Cyborg.

"No," added Starfire.

Robin frowned and said, "I see. Allow me to bring you all up to speed…"

He paused for a moment dramatically and then shouted, "Today is *Sports Day*! *SPPOOOOOORRRRTSS DAAAAAAAAAY!* Why do I even bother printing flyers?!"

The other Titans glanced around the room and noticed for the first time several dozen pieces of paper taped to the wall. Each one had SPORTS DAY written on it. The Titans shrugged and turned their attention back to Robin.

"Today we will be playing the world's most popular sport. We will be playing *fútbol*!"

Cyborg immediately lifted his right hand in the air in a classic football-trophy pose.

"Football! I *love* football!" he said as he threw his imaginary football. *"Touchdown!"*

Starfire reached behind the couch and grabbed a football helmet. She placed it on top of her head.

"Hut, hoot-hoot, hut hut hut, hiker!" she cried out as she ran across the room.

Beast Boy jumped off the couch and chased after Starfire. Raven jumped happily in the air to cheer on her teammates.

Robin frowned and said, "I didn't say we're playing *football*!"

Beast Boy paused to stare at Robin and said, "Uh, I'm pretty sure you did, bro."

"No, bro," insisted Robin. "I said we're playing *fútbol*!"

Cyborg again hoisted his imaginary football and declared, "Football! I *love* football! *Touchdown!*"

"Hut, hoot-hoot, hut hut hut, hiker!" added Starfire as she resumed running around the room.

"No! We are *not* playing football!" Robin screamed.

Beast Boy scratched his head and said, "I'm so confused, bro."

"We are playing *fútbol*..." Robin began, and then noticing the puzzlement on the faces of his teammates, he added, "...*also* known as *soccer*!"

The other four Titans instantly groaned in dismay.

"*Boooo!*" yelled Cyborg. "Nobody cares about soccer!"

"It is the *most* tedious of athletic events," added Starfire.

"It's just people kicking a ball and then pretending to be hurt!" protested Beast Boy.

Raven moved closer to Beast Boy and said, "I don't like sock-*her*, either. I prefer sock-*him*!"

With that, Raven magically formed a giant fist and clobbered Beast Boy with it.

BLAM!

Beast Boy was knocked across the room.

"*Owwww!*" he cried out.

Raven smiled widely and said, "Sock-*him*, not sock-*her*. Get it?"

Robin continued to lecture the Titans and said, "Around the world, *fútbol* ignites the passions of the soul. It can bring a nation together…or tear it apart. *Most* important, it is a metaphor for the miracle of life!"

"Are we still talking about soccer?" asked a puzzled Cyborg.

Robin jumped up and down and screamed,

"Stop calling it soccer! It's fútbol*!"*

"You know, I've always thought there's something sinister about soccer," said Raven. "How can people get so worked up over a ball?"

Starfire nodded in agreement and said, "It does seem unlikely that a dull game could inspire such intense emotions, Robin."

Robin ignored their comments and said, "*Fútbol* is a beautiful game! Now say it, and let it live in your hearts! *Fútbol!*"

"Football?" said Cyborg tentatively.

"No! *Fútbol*," said Robin with disgust.

"*Fútbol.*" said Starfire hopefully, but a little unsure.

"With passion!" urged Robin.

"*Fútbol!*" bellowed Beast Boy.

"*That's* starting to sound international!" Robin said encouragingly.

"Sock-*him*," said Raven with a smile.

Raven used her magic to once again crush Beast Boy with a giant fist.

"*Owwww!* Quit it!" cried Beast Boy.

Raven chuckled quietly and said proudly, "I'm hilarious."

"Great energy, Titans!" Robin called out as he sprang into action. "Now let's *take the field*!" He pulled a grapnel launcher from his Utility Belt and shot it at the ceiling. Seconds later, he was swinging on a line through the air.

BLAM!

He crashed through the living room window and plummeted down the side of Titans Tower.

The other Titans shrugged with boredom and took the elevator to the ground floor.

CHAPTER 2

Minutes later, the heroes were gathered on the lush green lawn outside Titans Tower. Each Titan was wearing a headband, soccer shorts, and a T-shirt with a large *T* on it.

"We look like the athletics professionals!" observed Starfire.

Beast Boy turned to Cyborg and said, "Ha-ha, I got shin pads, yo! Kick me as hard as you can!"

Cyborg shook his head doubtfully and said, "Seems like a bad idea, bro."

"C'mon, I won't feel a thing!" insisted Beast Boy. "It's shin armor!"

"Well, okay…" said Cyborg.

KER-BLAM!

Cyborg's metallic foot slammed into Beast Boy's leg.

"*Owwwwww!* My shin!" Beast Boy cried out as he doubled over in pain. "You broke my shin!"

Starfire ran over to Beast Boy.

"I, too, wish to test the shin armor!" she said as she kicked Beast Boy's other leg.

WHAM!

"Ow! Ow! Ow!" Beast Boy wailed in pain as he crumpled to the ground. "These shin pads aren't guarding anything...not a thing!"

"You guys playing sock-*him*?" Raven asked. "Cool."

POW!

Raven created a magical fist that slammed into Beast Boy.

Whimpering and crying as he crawled along the ground, Beast Boy said, "I can't feel my toes...."

Robin raised his hand and said, "Enough horseplay, guys."

His teammates turned to listen to him.

"Let's get to the basics," said Robin. "Because no one plays soccer in our country, I've had this ball shipped to us from halfway around the world." He held a shiny black-and-white soccer ball in his hands. His teammates' eyes widened.

Cyborg leaned closer and observed, "*Ooooooh*, what a good-looking ball!"

"A collection of pentagons and hexagons forming a sphere!" said Starfire.

"It's made out of science, yo!" declared Beast Boy.

"Stylish," admitted Raven.

"It's true," said Robin with pride. "The *fútbol* is the most stylish piece of equipment in all of sports."

He pointed toward the steel-frame soccer

goal at the end of the field.

"Now, this is an easy game to learn. You just have to put the ball into the goal."

"No problem," said Beast Boy as he grabbed the ball from Robin's hands and threw it into the goal.

"Swish! Two points!" Beast Boy called out as he danced around the field to celebrate.

"*No* points!" declared Robin. "You can't use your *hands*!"

"*What?!*" asked a shocked Beast Boy.

"Things just got *super* weird!" said Cyborg.

"How does one manipulate the ball, without using the hands?" asked a puzzled Starfire.

"*Fút-bol!*" said Robin triumphantly.

"Oh, I get it!" said Beast Boy with a smile. "Dudes, we use our foots!"

Raven, who was hovering a few feet above

the ground, said, "But I don't have feet."

"Yes, you *do*!" said Robin as he pointed to Raven's two feet that were peeking out beneath her cloak.

Raven lifted her cloak an inch, revealing her feet.

"Oh, yeah. Forgot about those," she said.

"Now, pay attention as I demonstrate a proper *fútbol* kick," said Robin.

He kicked the ball into the goal.

"There, I've scored a goal in the appropriate *fútbol* style," said Robin. "Now let's celebrate by saying 'goal' as long as possible."

"Goal," said Raven.

Robin shook his head in disdain and asked, "What is this, baseball?"

Beast Boy transformed himself into a green basset hound and howled, *"Goooaaalll!"*

"Not long enough!" said Robin.

Starfire's voice soared up and down between two octaves as she sang out, "The *GoAaAaAaAal*!"

"Unacceptable!" declared Robin with a serious frown.

"GOOOOOOOOO OOOOAAAAAAAAAAAAAAAAAAALLLLLL!" bellowed Cyborg.

"That's what I'm talking about!" yelled Robin. "Now let's *fut* this *bol*!"

For the next hour, the Titans scampered from one end of the field to the other, sweating and straining under Robin's guidance.

"Unlock the power of your feet!" yelled Robin. "Kick, kick, kick!"

When the Titans paused for a second, Robin started screaming, "Never stop *running*. Always chase that ball all over the place like a crazy dog!"

The Titans barked like dogs as they chased the ball.

"Now we need to practice being hurt," said Robin. "It's important to act injured when touched by another player to draw penalties. *Overacting* is encouraged!"

Robin reached out his finger to lightly tap Beast Boy's shoulder.

"Owwwwwww!" cried out Beast Boy as he fell to the ground and moaned in pain.

"Good work," said Robin. "And now, your final task is to become *sore losers*."

The Titans turned to notice that Silkie, Starfire's mutant moth larva pet, had wandered onto the soccer field. The little creature walked over to the soccer ball and nudged it into the goal.

The outraged Titans hurled chairs and chunks of grass from the soccer field at the startled creature. Silkie fled the field in tears. The Titans were quick learners when it came to being sore losers.

"Wow! *Fútbol* isn't boring at all," declared Cyborg. "In fact, I feel like I'm standing on the precipice of greatness! I am a pillar of light in a world of darkness!"

Beast Boy reached both arms high above his head and shouted, "We're taking our first steps into a new life, bro! The *fútbol liiiiiiife!*"

Starfire began sobbing and then suddenly started laughing hysterically. *"Ha-ha-ha-ha!"* she yelled. "Why are we feeling such intense emotions?"

Raven frowned and said, "These feelings, they don't make sense—"

"Of *course* they do!" Robin interrupted as he juggled a soccer ball with his knees.

"This beautiful, magical ball was the key to unlocking our passions!"

Raven continued to look doubtful as she slowly said, "Still...something about this feels unnatural."

Robin kicked the ball through the air. It landed on top of Raven's head.

As she balanced the ball above her, Raven

suddenly smiled and said, "But I can't argue with my feelings! *Goooooooooooooooooooooooaaa aaaaaaaaaaaallllllllllllllllllllll!*"

CHAPTER 3

The next day, after Raven finally stopped yelling *"Goal,"* the Titans were gathered around the kitchen table in Titans Tower. Robin was pouring cereal into a bowl, and Raven was floating in front of the refrigerator.

"Raven, could you pass the milk?" asked Robin.

"Sure thing," said Raven as she reached into the refrigerator. Instead of using her hands, though, she knocked her foot against the milk carton and kicked it across the room. After the milk carton landed on Robin's head, he bounced it against his knee to pour milk into his bowl. He then kicked the container back into the refrigerator.

The other Titans jumped into the air and cheered, *"Goaaaaalll!"*

Beast Boy walked past Cyborg to grab a banana. His arm briefly brushed up against Cyborg's left leg.

"Excuse me, bro…" apologized Beast Boy.

Cyborg howled in pain and tumbled backward. He landed on the kitchen floor with a *thud.*

"*Whoaaaa!*" he wailed as he clutched his knee. "The pain! *The pain!*"

TWEET!

Robin blew a whistle and called out, "Red card! Penalty on Beast Boy!"

"A red card?!" yelled an outraged Beast Boy. "You've got to be kidding me! I barely *touched* him!"

Robin pointed to the living room and shouted, "I don't want to hear it! You're *out of here!*"

Grumbling under his breath, Beast Boy stalked out of the kitchen. "Unbelievable!" he muttered. "You need to get your eyes checked!"

Starfire ignored her teammates and started running in circles around the living room couch. She increased her speed until she became a blur of pink and purple.

"I never want to stop the running!" she said happily. "I feel so invigorated!"

Raven magically appeared above the couch and called out, "We have *never* lived our lives with such emotion!"

Robin reached for the soccer ball and held it over his head. "That's right!" he said. "We've all been invigorated by this magical little *fútbol*."

The other Titans gasped in horror and pointed toward Robin.

"What?" asked Robin. "What did I do?"

"Your *hands*!" shouted Cyborg.

"You're using your *hands*, bro!" yelled Beast Boy.

"Yikes!" said Robin as he immediately dropped the ball.

Seconds later, the Titans gasped again when a crack appeared in the ball after it hit the floor.

"Now you've done it!" said Cyborg in an anguished voice.

Raven leaned forward to study the ball. The crack appeared to be growing larger. "Whoa," she said as the ball began to wiggle and the crack widened. "What's that?"

Robin reached out with his bo staff and pulled apart the two halves of the ball. The

Titans were astonished to see that there was a small, round, purple creature nestled inside the ball. The creature had two large yellow eyes and a tuft of blond hair on top of his head.

"Thank you! Thank you!" he said. Noticing the shocked looks on the faces of the Titans, the creature continued, "I'm a Soccer Troll, and I can't tell you how long I've been trapped inside this soccer ball!"

"You mean *fútbol*, bro," corrected Beast Boy smugly.

"Who calls it a *fútbol*?!" asked the creature. "This is a soccer ball!"

"And what do Soccer Trolls do?" asked Robin.

"We are magical beings that evoke intense passions in anyone who is near us."

"So you guys use *magic* to get people to like soccer?" asked Cyborg with disgust.

"Absolutely," confirmed the Soccer Troll.

"That's incredible," said Robin. "But how did you get stuck inside a soccer ball?"

"I was trapped by the Soccer Overlords!" the creature said sadly.

"But why?" asked Starfire.

"Because watching people kick a ball and pretend to be hurt is the most boring thing in the *world*!" said the Soccer Troll.

Beast Boy nodded in agreement and added, "Yeah, that's what I said!"

"The Soccer Overlords knew the only way to create interest in their dull sport was to trap one of my people in every ball. We have to use our magic to get people excited about soccer!"

"No wonder the game stirs such proud but unearned emotions!" said Cyborg.

"What a monstrous sport!" muttered Raven.

Robin frowned and said, "It's time for people to see soccer for what it really is. Soccer Troll, take us to the Soccer Overlords!"

CHAPTER 4

As commanded, the Soccer Troll accompanied the Teen Titans down a very long tunnel that led to a giant, secret cavern far below the surface of the earth. When the Titans emerged from the tunnel, they found themselves standing in the middle of the largest soccer field they had ever seen. Laughing and howling Soccer Trolls filled the grandstands that lined the field. An ornate golden throne stood at one end of the field, surrounded by flaming torches and skulls. On top of the throne sat a giant, purple, fleshy monster. Atop his monstrous head, he wore an oddly shaped soccer-ball hat with giant antlers on each side of it.

"That must be the king of the Soccer Overlords," whispered Robin.

With an evil grin, the giant purple monster chortled and said, "Well done, Titans; you've uncovered my centuries-old plot to make soccer interesting!"

Robin stepped forward and said, "Give it up, Overlord! No more using magic to trick people into liking soccer!"

"I must, or the sport would never survive!" protested the Overlord. "It's just people kicking a ball and pretending to be hurt!

128

Who would watch that?!"

"One way or another, we're going to settle this!" threatened Robin.

The Overlord grinned and hopped off his throne. "Well then, how about settling it on the field?" he taunted, placing a ball under his giant foot. "One goal, sudden death!"

Suddenly, more Soccer Overlords surrounded the Titans. The Overlords expertly kicked soccer balls to one another.

"If we win, you call back all the Soccer Trolls and—" Robin began.

Before Robin could finish, the Overlords quickly scored a goal.

"Goooaaaallll!" yelled the Overlords.

"They're really good," said Cyborg in an openly worried voice.

"You lose, Titans!" said the Soccer Overlord with a laugh. "Time to die!"

Robin struck a pose and said, "You're forgetting one thing. The Titans are *sore losers*! Let's take down the Overlords! Titans: *Goooooaaaaalll!*"

"Yaaaaaaah!" shouted Beast Boy as he transformed himself into a giant green gorilla. He reached forward with his paws to wrench

free a big chunk of the grassy soccer field. As he did that, he knocked over two Overlords.

Robin picked up a series of lawn chairs and threw them at the Overlords. The purple creatures backed away in fear.

Raven created a giant magical fist and pounded the soccer goal into pieces.

Starfire flew circles around four Overlords, blasting them with starblasts from her eyes.

Cyborg bumped into the king of the Overlords. The creature then fell on the ground, clutching his knee.

"Ow, my leg, my leg!" he cried in fake pain.

"Red card!" yelled Robin.

"Okay, okay, you win," protested the Overlord as he stood up. "I'll call back my Soccer Trolls!"

With a victorious cheer, the Titans charged

at the Overlord and knocked him over again. Beast Boy started biting him. Robin smacked him with his bo staff. Raven bashed him with her trusty magical fist. Cyborg kicked him with his metal foot. And Starfire punched him enthusiastically.

"I said you win, you win..." protested the weary creature.

Slowly, the Titans stopped pummeling the Overlord.

"This is *so* boring," observed Beast Boy.

"I've got an idea," said Cyborg with a smile.

"Let's go bowling!"

The Titans watched with excitement as Cyborg reached into his mechanical torso and extracted a shiny bowling ball.

"Oops," said Cyborg as the bowling ball slipped from his fingers and crashed to the ground.

CRAAAACK!

The Titans watched with astonishment as the ball split open and a large brown turkey emerged from within the shards of the broken bowling ball.

"Who are you?" asked Robin.

"I'm a magical bowling turkey!" announced the bird. "Gobble, gobble, gob—"

KER-BLAM!

Before the turkey could finish its third 'gobble,' Cyborg blasted it with the sonic cannon mounted on his arm.

"Back to the Tower to watch TV?" asked Cyborg.

The other four Titans smiled and nodded.

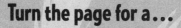

Turn the page for a...

BONUS ACTIVITY

The Teen Titans chase Control Freak into an arcade, where he zaps them back into a video game!

Draw the 8-bit Titans
battling pixelated villains.

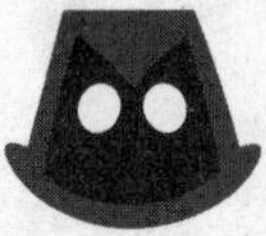

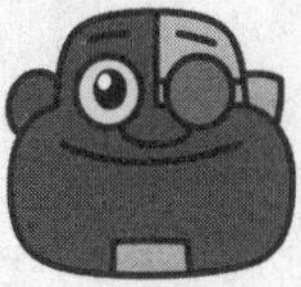

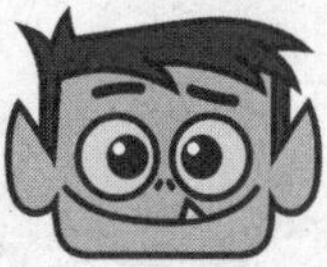

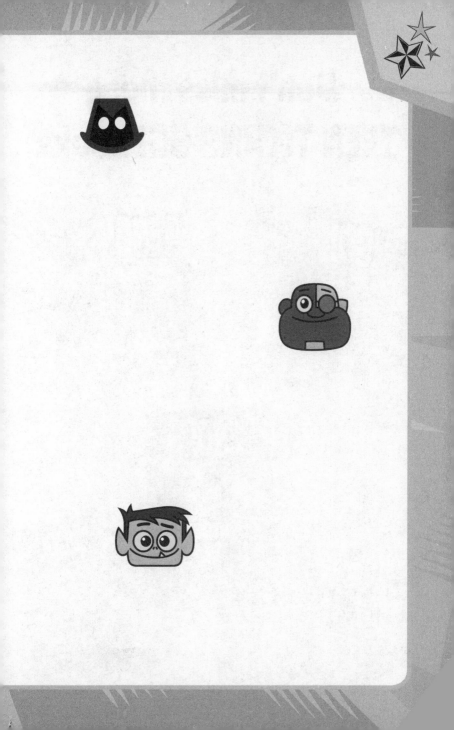

Don't miss these
TEEN TITANS GO! books.